Driving on MARS

by Mary Kay Carson

 HOUGHTON MIFFLIN   BOSTON

The landscape of Mars is bleak and rocky. The bottom of this photo shows the Pathfinder and one of its open doors.

Red Planet Rover

It was a chilly summer day on the planet Mars. The temperature was only 8°F. Mars looked like a desert of reddish rocks and dirt under a pinkish sky.

There on the gravelly plain rested a machine called a
lander. Its open doors looked like three petals. The
lander, called Pathfinder, had been sent from Earth to land
on Mars. Anchored inside Pathfinder was a robot car, or
rover, named Sojourner. Sojourner was the size of a
microwave oven and had six wheels. It was the first
moving vehicle ever to visit another planet.

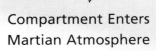
Pathfinder's Mission

It had taken three years and $150 million to build and launch the rover and its lander. This was fast and cheap compared to other Mars missions. Many people said the mission would never work. But on December 2, 1996, Pathfinder was put on a rocket and launched into space.

Pathfinder's voyage to Mars took seven months. On July 4, 1997, it arrived at the red planet. To save money, the National Aeronautics and Space Administration (NASA) had designed Pathfinder for a crash landing. As Pathfinder entered the atmosphere of Mars, its parachute opened. The speed of the spacecraft slowed to 150 miles per hour.

Parachute
Separates

Parachute
Opens

Heat Shield
Separates

Pathfinder
Drops on Tether

This drawing shows
Pathfinder's descent
to the surface of
Mars on July 4, 1997.

Radar Senses
Ground

Braking Rockets
Ignite

Air Bags
Inflate

Air Bags Deflate

Air Bags Pull Back

Pathfinder in
Final Position

Ten seconds before Pathfinder hit the ground, its giant air bags inflated. Pathfinder slammed into the ground at thirty miles per hour and bounced forty feet into the air. It bounced sixteen times, like a giant beach ball. Then the lander rolled to a stop in the red dust.

Each of the air bags that protected Pathfinder as it landed was made of five layers of a special material.

Members of the Pathfinder team cheer
after Pathfinder lands safely on Mars.

Cheers and yells filled the Mission Operations room of the Jet Propulsion Laboratory, a California company that is part of NASA. NASA scientists had a lot to celebrate that Fourth of July.

Pathfinder's airbags let out their air. The doors of the spacecraft opened. Sojourner was inside, safe and sound. Pathfinder pointed its antennas toward Earth. It radioed home. Then it started carrying out one of its main tasks—snapping pictures.

Pathfinder's pictures soon reached Earth. They were the first pictures taken of Mars in more than twenty years.

One of Pathfinder's first pictures shows the lander's deflated air bags, and the Martian landscape beyond.

In the Driver's Seat

Shortly after landing, Sojourner's motors began to whir. The rover slowly moved down a ramp and onto Mars. Its wheels left tread marks in the dust.

Sojourner didn't move on its own, though. Brian Cooper decided how Sojourner would move. Cooper is a computer engineer. He wrote the computer program that controlled Sojourner. He was also Sojourner's lead driver. Cooper's job was to control Sojourner as it explored Mars.

The rover Sojourner rolls onto Martian soil.

Controlling a robot rover on Mars was a dream come true for Brian Cooper. As a kid in California, he loved video games and toy cars operated by remote control. He read science fiction stories about robots and talking computers. When he saw Neil Armstrong walk on the moon in 1969, Brian decided to become a pilot or an astronaut.

When Cooper grew up, he joined the Air Force. But poor eyesight kept him from becoming a pilot. He was disappointed but still interested in machines. "I built my first robot in college," Cooper said. "I used it to explore my living room."

Brian Cooper was Sojourner's lead driver.

Using a sandbox, scientists practiced what would happen after Pathfinder landed on Mars.

After college, Cooper went to work at NASA testing robot vehicles, including Sojourner. The Sojourner drivers couldn't go to Mars to test their rover. So they built a place on Earth that looked like Mars. It was a giant sandbox filled with rocks just like the ones on Mars. Sojourner's drivers spent a lot of time practicing in the sandpit.

Now it was time to put the practice to work. Cooper sat in front of a computer. The screen showed Sojourner parked near the lander on Mars. The scientists wanted Sojourner to examine a colorful rock nearby. They named the rock Barnacle Bill. Cooper wore 3-D goggles. He operated a joystick that moved Sojourner on the computer screen. Using these instruments, Cooper felt like he was on Mars. He could see how big the rocks were and how far away they were from Sojourner. Cooper began to weave the little rover around the rocks.

Brian Cooper guided Sojourner using 3-D goggles and a computer wth a joystick.

Sojourner's main instrument identified the chemicals in Martian rocks.

12

Controlling a rover from 119 million miles away was not easy. It took each message about eleven minutes to reach Mars from Earth. If Sojourner were headed for a cliff, it would fall off by the time it got a message telling it to stop. Cooper had to use the computer to plan safe routes for Sojourner.

This solar panel provided power for Sojourner in daytime.

Scientists designed and built Sojourner's antennas.

Tiny heaters and very lightweight insulation protected Sojourner from low temperatures of -127°F.

Barnacle Bill

This is what images from Mars looked like on Brian Cooper's computer screen.

The Pathfinder's pictures of Mars showed where Sojourner was. The computer used these pictures to create a landscape just like Mars. The landscape made Mars look like the real thing on Cooper's screen. Once Cooper had the steps of a safe route planned, he sent them to Sojourner.

Barnacle Bill

Yogi

After Sojourner studied Barnacle Bill, it moved
on to a rock that scientists named Yogi.

Eleven minutes after Cooper sent his commands,
Sojourner turned and headed toward Barnacle Bill. The
rock was only ten feet away. But Sojourner needed to be
right up against the rock to study it. The rover moved
slowly closer to the rock. Full stop! It was a perfect
parking job. A special tool on Sojourner pressed against
Barnacle Bill and began studying the rock.

Results of the Mission

The Mars Pathfinder mission was a huge success. The lander was designed to work for only one month. Sojourner was designed to work for only one week. But Sojourner kept working, and Pathfinder kept sending back pictures—16,500 in all. When Pathfinder's batteries finally died on September 27, 1997, Sojourner lost touch with Earth.

Scientists learned a lot about Mars in those three months. They learned what each rock was made of. They also learned about the temperature and wind patterns of Mars. Most important, they learned that a lander and rover could explore Mars successfully. More missions to Mars were sure to come.

A large team of scientists worked hard to make Pathfinder and Sojourner's mission successful.